You Come from Love

This book is a work of fiction. The names, characters and events in this book are the products of the author's imagination or are used fictitiously. Any similarity to real persons living or dead is coincidental and not intended by the author.

You Come from Love

www.GatekeeperPress.com

Copyright © 2022 by Adam Motz

All rights reserved. Neither this book, nor any parts within it may be sold or reproduced in any form or by any electronic or mechanical means, including information storage and retrieval systems, without permission in writing from the author. The only exception is by a reviewer, who may quote short excerpts in a review.

Library of Congress Control Number: 2022947392

ISBN (hardcover): 9781662936234

You Come from Love

Written by Adam Motz

Illustrated by Jordan Aspiras

Motz Books

*To Reve and Sky—
our dreams come true.*

I tell you, my child,
that you come from love.

A love that surrounds you,
around and above

Love from the universe,
love from the stars

Love from the God
that made you who you are

Love from the motherland, heartland, and earth

Love from the Song
they all sang at your birth

Love from your ancestors,
love from your tribe

Love from your family
that brought you to life.

Love that will lift you,
again and again

Love that will carry you,
now 'til the end

Love from the promise
that brought us to you

You come from love...

and love comes from you!

Printed in the USA
CPSIA information can be obtained
at www.ICGtesting.com
LVHW061627290923
759564LV00071B/36